PLEASE

Poetic Expressions of the Human Heart

By Joyce G. Moore

Please Hear Our Cries
Poetic Expressions of the Human Heart

by
Joyce G. Moore

ISBN: 978-1-931259-08-8

For information contact:
Joyce G. Moore
Post Office Box 1683
Marietta, GA 30061

Printed in USA

Dedication

This publication is dedicated to all who are diligently working every day to peacefully survive in today's evolving world. To all who "Hear Our Cries" and respond appropriately, I extend my heartfelt thanks. To my devoted family and friends, I thank you for encouraging me in all of my many endeavors. You are the 'wind beneath my wings'.

This dedication is extended to my loving parents, my forefathers and all who have paved the way for us to have the opportunity to live in a civil and humane society. Let not their work be in vain. In their honor, may we all strive to keep hope alive.

"Without Hope People Perish"

Please Hear Our Cries
Poetic Expressions of the Human Heart

Our human emotions can run very deep, ranging from joy to despair. The human heart can serve as our radar detector. It senses our feelings as they come flooding in, and an alarm is sounded. When this alarm sounds, we may go into a "flight or fight mode". This alarm may also cause us to become still because we are frozen, and we are attempting to gather our thoughts. Humans are complex beings, and we think and respond in different unique ways.

The poetic expressions in this publication reflect the vast array of feelings to which so many can truly relate to. There may also be poetic expressions that elicit empathy regarding the plights of others. Life takes us on a journey involving so many diverse situations and an endless array of emotions. There are trials and tribulations of various degrees that we must continue to navigate.

Our ability to express our emotions provides us an opportunity to free ourselves of some of these pent-up feelings that need to be shared and resolved.

To the 'die-hard poets', you will find that the expressions in this publication do not adhere to scholarly forms. They are written purely from the heart and from many years of interacting with others who are experiencing life in its pure and honestly raw settings.

Each of you are invited to enjoy the messages and the intended blessings, and hopefully to expand your insight into a wider variety of human emotional conditions, through the vehicle of poetic expressions.

PLEASE HEAR OUR CRIES
Poetic Expressions of the Human Heart

Joyce G. Moore

Table of Contents

Lord, Please Hear Our Cries
Help Us All to Rise

When we feel the burdens of life
becoming too heavy to carry,
Please Hear Our Cries.

When we see no way to restore hope
here on this earth,
Please Hear Our Cries.

When we can't seem to escape
so much sadness and pain,
Please Hear Our Cries

When we have done all that we know to do,
and it is still not enough,
Please Hear Our Cries.

When we forget to turn to you
during our times of trouble,
Please Hear Our Cries.

When we think that our prayers
have gone unanswered,
Please Hear Our Cries.

Please Hear Our Cries
Please Hear Our Cries
Please Hear Our Cries
Help Us All to Rise

Me, In Six Words

I'm Me both inside and out.

I dream. Then I take action.

Bad fall opened my life's appreciation.

Claiming the good. Discarding the bad.

No lottery wins. Wining at life.

Happiness lives within my loving heart.

Born again in my early seventies.

Same name but different life goals.

Loving Me, no matter what happens.

I'm still a work in progress.

I'm Going to Get It Straight

I have a figure flaw.
It's called being overweight.
It's causing me a personal problem.
I can't seem to get it straight.

I'm trying to manage
to rearrange my hectic life.
Trying to find the solution
to cutting down on so much strife.

Some say that it has much to do
with the foods that I eat.
I have personally determined
that I have this theory beat.

I know that lack of exercise
is really at the core.
Too often I get busy
and don't enter that exercise door.

I know I have a figure flaw
and it is about being overweight.
I don't need this problem.
So, I'm going the get it straight.

A Child's Prayer

Now I lay me down to sleep.

I pray the Lord my soul to keep.

May all my dreams be the best.

I will now get my rest.

When I awake to a new day,

Please watch over me while I work and play.

Lord, Hear My Prayer.

AMEN

I Am, I Have, I Must, I Can, I Will, I Know

I <u>am</u> too important to let my life drift by.

I <u>have</u> too much to share to live without a care.

I <u>must</u> continue to live life with much meaning every day.

I <u>can</u> offer special gifts of mine:
My talents, my time, my grace divine.

I <u>will</u> practice unique ways to make this world a better place.

I <u>know</u> too much good to keep it hidden.
For such behavior by me is really forbidden.

Flea Market

It is called a "Flea Market",
although they have no fleas to sell.
Wonder how that idea ever came about?
Well, do all things have to have a reason
that others can figure out.

The "Bed Bug Market"
may have had less of an appeal.
The thought of either name
may cause some to
let out a high pitch squeal.

So, when deciding on a certain name,
I'll come to one's defense.
You really don't have to have
a reason to keep us in suspense.

Too Late for Vindication

Some lives begin with a strange twist.
Hence, feeling cursed while on this earth.
Then comes vindication after death.
It's too late for them to feel the love,
'cus the spirit has moved on up above.

Into my mind the thought just doesn't fit.
Some things the human brain just can't get.
It is so hard to understand
why there was no justice before being put to rest.
This good human was put to a cruel earthly test.

When joining in to say goodbye,
in honor of the departed,
at least let's begin embracing peace.
It helps to heal a broken heart
when we play an active part.

Please Hear Our Cries

Looking for a "New Song" to Sing

Some days we wake up wondering
what the new day will bring.
We are seeking to do something different
and looking for a "New Song" to sing.

The old ways and songs no longer serve
the body, mind nor soul.
Now is time to make some changes
and rip away the old.

It will take some time to prepare
to retrain the human mind.
It will help to identify what, who, when
and how – as I attempt changes to define.

I am looking for a "New Song"
that just may be circling in my head.
I will sing this happy new song
from the time I wake up, until I go to bed.

It Is Up to You

We have been given this life
to do the best that we could.
We could throw it away
or do something good.

We could make another person happy
or make someone sad.
What have you done so far
with this life that you have had?

you could wear a smile upon your face
or wear an unpleasant frown.
You could lift someone up
or help keep someone down.

What are you doing with your special gift
of your marvelous life today?
Please do something really good
and not waste your life away.

Searching

I've spent a lifetime searching
for happiness just for me.
It may be hiding out
in places that I can't see.

Thumbing through book pages,
and under leaves pilled so high.
Searching everywhere on earth
and even looking up to the sky.

Finding what I'm searching for
has eluded me to this very day.
May not know it when I find it,
for no clues have even come my way.

A little bit of happiness would feel
soooooo good right about now.
Tomorrow I'll resume the search,
hoping to find happiness somehow.

In the meantime, I'll curl up
with a good book and a cup of tea.
I will enjoy the peace and contentment
that comes from being alone with me.

~~~~~~

Oh, this is happiness.
I've been living with it all the time.

Too Often

Too often when I cry
no one sees my tears.

Too often when I worry
no one feels my stress.

Too often when I am in pain
no one feels my hurt.

Too often when I am happy
no one observes my smile.

Too often when I just want to be alone
everyone won't let me be.

Issue After Issue

Issue after issue
I need a tissue to dry my tears away

A boat load of tears may sink my boat
causing me to drown.

My sorrows creep in over unresolved life's events
that should never be.

There are so many simple things that could be solved
with sheer common sense.

Jumping through "Hoops" and too much "Red Tape"
being required to accomplish simple task.

Issue after issue causing too much pain.
It could drive a person insane.

~~~~~~~~~~~~~~~~~~

Please Hear Our Cries

Step Into My Personal World

Step into my personal world.
Feel the tightness of my shoes.
Know how I feel when living in a world
with so much bad news.

The bunions on my feet have grown
from constant pressure and wear.
Looking in the mirror I see a reflection
of how I've lost my hair.

I constantly sit in self-isolation in futile attempts
to really compose myself.
To help relieve some pressure,
I remove my shoes and place them on the shelf.

Step into my personal world
and then feel this pressure on you.
Once in my shoes you'll understand
why I feel as I do.

Who Do We Blame?

Who do we blame:

When the mop doesn't mop

When the sweeper doesn't sweep

When the pick doesn't pick

When the rake doesn't rake

When the brush doesn't brush

When the alarm doesn't alarm

When the baker doesn't bake

When the teacher doesn't teach

When the preacher doesn't preach

~~~~~~~~~~~

Who do we really blame?

A Rattle in My Brain

Living in a world
that appears to have gone insane.
At times it feels as if a rattle
has gone off in my brain.

There are many pebbles
moving around in my weary head.
Often the solution is to go
and jump into my comfortable bed.

After a good sound sleep
I hope the pebbles will settle down.
Must clear my head
of this rattling sound.

Sleep for me is a is a natural way
to quickly renew.
So, I turn to what I have learned
that has come to my rescue.

Plan for Happiness and Joy

Most plans must be made
for things to really be.
Some things don't always happen
just because we want them to.

We must make plans for such things
as happiness and joy.
Make plans for things to erase
the sadness and tears.

Make plans to connect with people
and explore places that create
those good memories to behold.
This is priceless like silver and gold.

We make plans that keep us living
the great lives that we deserve.
Remember, if is to be,
"It is up to you and me".

Loyal Friends

Loyal friends are gifts to us
from a loving universe.
Loyal friends are priceless –
to be cherished and adored.

Friends can live close or reside far away.
No matter where they are
their friendship can remain.

Nurture their friendship
to keep the bond true and alive.
Loyal friends will hear you
when you need a listening ear just to survive

They will be there
to help you through those dark times.
So, nurture your loyal friends
until the very end..

Stop Running and Sit for A Spell

Take time to sit.
What are you running from?
Is it just something living inside
and you are trying to run and hide?

No matter how fast you run
you have got to stop sometime.
Running is not always the thing to do.
You can't outrun you.

Take time to inventory your life.
Take note of what you are running from.
Are you running out of fear or is it for fun?
Are you just out for a daily run?

Give your legs a needed rest,
with a brain more energized,
with time to refuel and renew,
and think things through.

Scream to Release

When you need to release the daily pressures
and the intensities of life,
Scream!!!!!

When the burdens of life elevate
to a thunderous pitch,
Scream!!!!!

When the walls come closing in
and you can't manage to push them back,
Scream!!!!!

When others ignore your cry
for much needed help,
Scream!!!!!

When you are just looking
for something different to do,
Scream!!!!!

The lungs love a good old-fashioned release.
Scream!!!!!

Trust Me

When I confess my truth,
I ain't going to lie.
Trust me.

When I need to tell some things
you may not even want to hear.
Trust me.

When I need to share my pain and heart aches.
Trust me.

When I need to come out of hiding the real me.
Trust me.

Let me be my authentic self.
No desire to be anyone else.
Trust me.

Lack of trust makes us hide
and keep so many things inside.
Trust me.

Holidays

Holidays are times of celebrations
with diverse given names.
Holidays do not always coincide in bringing happiness
and a desire for celebrations to one and all .

Expectations and the anxiety of joining may bring stress
and sadness to their human heart.
So, please allow others the freedom to decide
by making it their personal call.

Infirmities of the Weak

No strengths do I possess
to make it in this world alone.
I may need helping hands
to reach out to me.
Or just may need a loving hand up
from time to time.
May even need a dollar
or sometimes I just need a dime.

I was not blessed
with a gift of a strong body nor mind.
Some fail to understand my infirmities
are certainly not my personal choice.
So, when I appear along your pathways of life,
try to understand
and help if you can.

`ᶜᶜᶜᶜᶜᶜᶜᶜᶜᶜᶜᶜᶜᶜ

Please Hear Our Cries

Foundation for Living

Every structure needs a solid foundation
to secure the building that is being created.

Every life placed upon this earth
also needs that solid foundation to safely survive.

One may add pillows of support
for added endurance and aesthetic appeal.

Make no mistake the structure will crumble
without strong support and if built on sinking sand.

So, secure your human structure with a solid foundation,
to assure that you will continue to firmly stand.

Together We Stand

Togetherness of ideas, ideals and quality of workmanship
must be included in the recipe for remaining united.

Together we stand
but divided we fall.
It takes good 'brick and mortar'
to build a solid secure wall.

When we all stand together and work for the common good,
good things will truly happen and work out as they should.

Confessions

Confessions are said to be "Good for the soul".
It may be true,
depending upon who you are confessing to.

It also depends on what or when.
How good will the soul feel
when the confession is finally through?

Is it taking place in a real "Confessional Booth"
or to a real trusted friend?
Or is it confessing to someone
who may cause you harm in the end?

The decision to confess is certainly up to you.
Just make sure you think it through before you do.

Pain As the Messenger

Pain flares up,
out of nowhere it seems.
It is delivering messages
for reasons of its own.

Learning to read the message
takes a special skill.
It may take a professional to understand
what it truly means.

Do not ignore the message
or the messenger of the pain.
Make it known that you are not complaining
but just explaining the pain that you feel.

Know You Are Not Alone

Know that when you are happy,
someone else is happy too.
Know that when you are sad,
someone else is sad too.
When you are going through rough times,
someone else is too.

Whatever you are going through, just remember
that you are not going through something alone.
No one monopolizes sadness or pain.
Every human condition is shared by someone else.
It may help a little by knowing
that you are not alone.

```````````````````````````

## Someone, Please Hear Our Cries
```````````````````````````

Second Thoughts

By having second thoughts,
sometimes it is what it takes
to avoid making too many mistakes.

Second thoughts may give us time
to make the better choice,
as we listen to our own more logical voice.

The first choice may be the choice
proving to be the best.
Having other choices puts the mind to rest.

Jumping to quick conclusions
is not a decisions maker's friend.
Decisions made in haste may be a disaster in the end.

Don't Always Ask Me Why

Please don't always ask me why.
My true answer may be a secret to keep.
So, the answer that I give may really be a lie.

I have my personal reasons
for doing the things that I do.
My way of doing things may be a mystery to you.
So rather than having to explain
I'd rather not come true.

Just don't always ask me why.
I'd rather not be forced to tell a lie.

At the Foot of the Mountain

I'm standing at the foot of the mountain,
getting ready to make this climb.
This is no tiny mountain.
It is also mighty mighty steep.

This is not my first climb
but I'm older than before.
This terrain is also much more rugged.
So, the journey may be rough.

Just like in our personal lives,
we must prepare for the mountain's climb.
We can't take the climb lightly,
or we may not make it through.

Prepare to Safely Stay the Course

When the course gets too rough,
remember to buckle up, slow down
and prepare to stay the course.

Keep your focus and keep looking ahead.
Look out for all the bumps in the road
and continue to slowly stay the course.

There also may be "potholes" along the way.
So, continue to stay focused
and cautiously stay the course.

The roads along the journey
have posted signs, warnings and alerts.
So, remember to abide by these rules of the road
as you prepare to stay the course.

Your destination may be near or ever so far.
Just stay focused on the roads
as you continue to safely
stay the course.

Pull Away

When things appear to be getting out of hand,
Pull away.

When "Social Media" has begun to personally affect you,
Pull away.

When you find yourself in a crowd of rule breakers,
Pull away.

When the pace of life is going too fast,
Pull away.

~~~~~~~~~~~~~~~~

As you take needed time to pull away,
just prepare to take a break, slow down, re-calibrate.
Take time for your own personal reflections
and slowly get back on the track that is meant for you.

Remember, They Don't Know You

When words spoken about you
defy the truth,
Remember, they don't know you.

When unkind and underserving
things are done to you,
Remember, they don't know you.

When strangers speak roughly
and unjustly to you,
Remember, they don't know you.

When folk on "Social Media"
wrongly attack your character,
Remember, they don't know you.

~~~~~~~~~~~~~~~

We are living in a world where we must continue
to believe in ourselves and continue to hold
our heads up high and maintain our dignity
through all the trials and tribulations.
Continue to know who you are and what you stand for.

Life Happens

Life does not flow
as we always wish.
So, be on guard for unwanted trials
to happen at any time.

Things could be going just great
or things could be going rough.
Just continue to maintain the fortitude
to continue to make it through.

Trust your instincts and this marvelous universe
to show you pathways to succeed.
Be still, be quiet and listen
to the message that you may need.

~~~~~~~~~~~~

Please Hear Our Cries

Customer Service

Customer service can be a joke.
Only it does not tend to make me laugh.
Getting some service by phone or in person
sometimes make me want to scream.

The "Pandemic" was once an excuse
for customer service being in short supply.
Now that things should be getting much better,
that excuse does no longer fly.

Now, to avoid being too annoyed,
expectations must be lowered
to keep from blowing my stack.
Now, when needing customer service,
I take a "Chill Pill" to keep my nerves in tack.

Don't Give Up

When situations have finally
gotten the best of you,
try taking a break and take time to renew.

It may not always be easy
to accomplish certain tasks.
Sometimes we must suit-up
and put on those gloves and mask.

We must do all that it takes
to get through the trenches of life.
Reach for those handy tools
to minimize so much misery and strife.

If anyone is able to see the job through,
you may be the only one.
So, re-energize with all your might.
Don't give up until the job is done.

The Pain Convention

Overnight the "Pain Convention" decided to convene.
My body is the site for this painful force.
I'm awakened with no warning
of the "Pain Agenda" for the day.
My body is the host
against its might or will.

The attendees move about my body
from place to place.
They move in unified teams
with no notice of where they will strike.
Pain gets my quick attention
and awaits my decisive response.
I'm being caught off-guard,
with no quick way to defend.

As an unwilling host
I must quickly fortify my resolve.
I offer "unpleasant snacks" that I have on hand
to help discourage the pain.
My goal is to be an ungracious host
and get the" Pain Convention" to rapidly go away.
By being a discourteous host
I hope this convention will swiftly end
and never come back again.

A Rebel with a Cause

The need to go along to accommodate
another's agenda
may not be the best for me.
My reasons are based on
the situation that I personally feel and see.

Some may call me "a rebel" but they fail to understand,
I'm really a decisive dissident with my own cause.
My freedom to make personal choices is a right
given to every woman and man.
I like deciding when my time could be better spent
by doing things that bring me greater joy.

So, learn to appreciate those who may not go along,
are not just being rebellious without a personal cause.
We have our own agenda.
So, please let us be.

No "Grudge-fest" for Me

Holding grudges is not too wise to do.
I find it counterproductive
and not good for me or you.

I work to abandon that old history
and those feelings of any discontent.
Thinking of all the good times
is energy more wisely spent.

Some unhappy events occurring in the past
were certainly out of my control.
Now I dwell on the good happenings of today.
I have released the sad days of old.

I am cherishing the current blessings
to store in my memory book.
It is more fun making my life a festival of joy.
I have let those who hurt me 'off of the hook'.

No "Grudge-fest for Me!

Things to Remember

Remember the good times
Remember the love
Remember the hugs
Remember the kisses
Remember the laughter
Remember the joy
Remember the peace
Remember the kindness
Remember the sunshine
Remember the moon
Remember the stars

~~~~

Remember the rain.
It can be rewarding
to wash away unwelcome pain.

Help

Help is a human need,
and it is essential to us all.
Acknowledging a need for help
takes pressure off the sensitive heart.

We can't be expected
to go it in this life alone.
Know to reach out when the time
signals that human need.

Help may be required
for giving or receiving.
Do not keep the need or offer for help
hidden secretly away.

Be brave and seek help when needed
to fend off a broken heart.
Help is a single word.
Now, add it to your 911 and 988.

....
Please Hear Ou Cries

Cast Away and Pop

Cast away those feelings
of sadness and discontent.
Now, pop those bubbles
of needless fear and doubt.

Cast away those feelings
of loneliness and isolation.
Pop those bubbles
of insecurity and shame.

Cast away those feelings
of inferiority and neglect.
Pop those bubbles
of ignorance and hate.

Cast away those things
that clutter up your life.
Pop those bubbles
that cause you sadness and strife.

~~~~~~~~

It is certainly up to you.

Eyes Wide Open

Knowing where I've been
is no mystery to me.
Knowing where I'm going
I must open my eyes to see.

Keeping my eyes wide open
is the wisest thing to do.
Keeping my eyes closed
I can't find my way through.

The obstacles along life's journey
can be wide. tall and deep.
These obstacles can confront you,
even in your sleep.

Now it is good to remember,
for sheer safety's sake,
always keep your eyes wide open,
especially when you are awake.
No chances should you take.

Fend Off the "Hounds"

The "Hounds" are on the hunt.
They are looking for their prey.
Seeking the innocent and confused,
who don't know to stay out of harm's way.

Sometimes they announce their arrival
with loud barking to create fear.
Then again, they use the silent tactic
and approach from the rear.

When their victims can't see or hear them,
they are caught off guard.
To fend off the evil enemy
you must be aware of existing fraud.

These "Hounds" will drain you dry.
They will use every trick in the book.
So, continue to be aware of the "Hounds",
who will attack, using hook and crook.

~~~~~~~~~~~~~~~~

Please Protect Us from the Hounds.
Please Hear Our Cries.

Folk In the Road

The highways of life
are designed for our travels.
Some roads are straight, winding,
narrow, mountainous and snaky.
Some roads are paved, graveled,
rough, bumpy and smooth.

The conditions of the roads
will determine our speed.
Going too fast or too slow
is an unsafe thing to do.
There are also those "Dead Ends"
and that "Folk in the Road" too.

We rely on navigational tools
to help direct us along the way.
What if they fail us
and the choice is ours to make?
When reaching the "Folk in the Road"
what direction will we take?

Must Repair a House Divided

A house too divided will not
continue to stand.
The cracks in the foundation
must immediately be repaired.
Using the best materials
and no expense must be spared.

Must unify the labor force
to expedite a uniform plan.
When everyone works together
the project will succeed.
The target date for completion will be
accomplished with deliberate speed.

So, if your house is divided,
draw up a detailed plan.
Gather all of your materials
and secure your labor force.
Quickly get to work,
to chart a successful course.

Planting Good Seeds

Good seeds planted in fertile soil
will sprout and grow.
It is hopeful that the crop will yield a return
of abundance and richness.

In your personal life, spend no time
planting seeds of regret or doubt.
Spend your time planting seeds
of faith, hope and charity.

Nourish your soil with much love, protection,
kindness, sunshine and rain.
Watch over your seeds as you witness the plants grow
and produce the fruits of your labor.

The day will come when you will witness
vegetation from the seeds that you did sow.
Harvest your crop and experience
Joy, happiness, harmony and peace.

Special Memories

Holding on to special memories
is what brings me much needed joy.
These memories help me
to fortify and enhance my soul.

It brings me extra unique pleasure to recall
those special good times from the past.
Embracing those joyous times
will never grow old.

I shall continue to build memories
to make my life worthwhile.
Finding that silver lining
adds much value to behold.

My daily ritual is to express
my genuine gratitude.
This practice reminds me that my life
and memories are as precious as gold.

Gratitude

An attitude of gratitude
will certainly serve you well.
It pays to acknowledge your appreciation
to those who have given to you.
Taking their "gifts" for granted
is not a grateful thing to do.

No matter how big or small
the "gift" might be,
it motivates the giver
to want to do even more.
Expressing gratitude for kind gestures
extended to you, increases your gratitude score.

Try a prayer of gratitude in place of a request.
It may intensify your blessings
that God will send your way.
So, maintain an attitude of gratitude
each and every day.

Tears

Tears serve a useful purpose to wash away
some sadness and emotional trauma.
There also may be tears
of happiness and joy.

There are feelings that come flooding in
that cannot always be explained.
Our feelings and emotions
truly have a mind of their own.

Release those emotions and allow
those tears to generously flow.
Let those tears run
their own cleansing course.

Lightly dry your eyes
when the tears are through.
Then receive the peace
as you take time to renew.

~~~~~~~~~~~~~~

Please Hear Our Cries

Severing Ties

When thoughts of things and/or people
are too unpleasant to endue,
it may be time to employ gentle ways
to distance yourself from them.

Severing ties may not be so easy for you.
Nevertheless, it may be the best thing to do.

Take time and sit a spell.
Think of ways to best move along.
Collect your thoughts and focus on the "why".
Be strong as you reflect on the "how".
The delivery of the message should be done
with kindness and grace.
Will it be done by phone, text, a letter,
or in person – face-to-face?

Some relationships are not truly meant to be.
Once the decision has finally been made,
be kind, be gentle and personally take the blame.
Severing ties must be done with tack,
and should never become a cruel game.

((((((((((((((((((((((((((((

Note: Understand the sensitive nature of some
when they feel a sense of rejection.
If this decision is not mutual, be aware of your approach.

Time to Stop and Reflect

Our human energy
may sometimes run low.
It causes us to move
at a pace that is unusually slow.

To keep from running out of needed fuel
we may need to modulate our speed.
Keep in mind, that the higher our speed,
the more fuel we will need.

So, do not continue to over-work
your body's precious engine.
Our body is our vehicle,
that needs servicing and fuel too.
Be aware of its needs
and when it is time to service you.

"The Unjustly Accused Blues"

Not until you've been
among the innocently accused,
will you truly understand
feeling the "Unjustly Accused Blues".

No crime having been committed
but cast behind steel bars,
while wearing prison attire,
and feeling hopelessness and despair.

Why don't they believe me
when I tell them the truth?
Mistaken identity is why I'm here.
My crime is looking like someone else.

What a broken system when the innocent
among us are wrongly cast away.
It can happen to anyone for a variety
of reasons on any given day.

God, please hear my cry.
Only you can save me.
I trust that you know the reason why.

Teach Me How to Love

In my defense, I don't know how to love.
I've never felt love before.
How could I learn to give
what I have never received?

I tend to pull away when others get too close.
I wish I could make them understand,
it is really me to blame and not them.

Is there a way to teach me how to love?
Then maybe it will not too late
to finally unravel my "loveless life".

By learning to begin to love myself,
this could be the start
of a magnificent life for me.

How does someone put into words
what other's feel naturally?
Please, someone magically appear
who will <u>Teach Me How to Love</u>.

Artificial Intelligence

Humans are being replace by technology invented by man.
Now we must navigate in a world
that some don't understand.

What does the future hold with all the changes in sight?
Now we have to "re-tool" our brain.
Just keeping up takes all our might.

Adapting to a new world is challenging to say the least.
We must apply ourselves if we don't want to
lose the battle to the "Artificial Intelligence Beast".

So, be aware that all technology is not your friend.
It may be smart enough to play a trick
and turn on you in the end.

Do the Best That You Can

Perfection in everything is not an absolute must,
unless it affects the health and safety of others and you.

For parents who have one of the hardest jobs around,
remove the pressure and do the best that you can.

For people in the workplace, know what is expected of you.
Then of course, continue to do the best that you can.

For friends, family and neighbors,
try to understand their unique personalities,
and then really do the best that you can.

\`((((((((((((((((((((((((((

When your best does not seem to be good enough,
know within your heart, that you <u>have</u> done your best,
when you have done the best that you could.

Where On Earth Is Utopia?

Will my search on earth yield any marvelous results?

With each sunrise I begin my sincere search.

I bravely approach strangers who are wearing a smile.
They too are clueless and would love to know.

I look to the vast blue sky and wonder if it is there.

Every friend and family member just gives me a smile.

The closest thing to Utopia must be in my heart.

The love and reverence for my *Divine Creator* is
"My Utopia Here on Earth".

Save Me from Me

So many bad habits have taken hold of me.
The list of unwanted habits
is long and fierce.

I am on a bumpy track, headed for self-destruction.
Self-help is beyond
my own ability and personal reach.

My past expressions of denial have driven others away.
I have been stubborn and determined
to do things my own way.

Needless to say and it is true,
"We do reap what we sow".
My challenging behavior has returned a life of dread.
I must get this thought into my own head.

~~~~~~~~~~~~~~~

Please Hear My Cries.
Who can save me from me?

Just Explaining – Not Complaining

When others ask how I'm doing,
I share things about what I'm going through.
Sharing such things as the situations in my life.
It may include the joy and the strife.

Sharing my life's events may sound to some,
like I am really complaining.
Some things are beyond their belief.
Sharing does bring me some relief.

~~~~~~~~~

Just Explaining – Not Complaining

Half-Full or Half-Empty

Some folks live seeing the glass half-full and not half-empty.
Some focus on filling another's half-empty vessel.

If you want a full glass let that choice be yours.
Filling another's vessel may not be their choice.

The beverage in that full vessel may not be to their taste.
The beverage may not be consumed and will go to waste.

It is best to honor another's request.
Do not force another to consume something
if they don't think it is the best.

~~~~~~~~~~~~

Half-Full or Half-Empty?
Just decide that only for yourself.

God Has a Sense of Humor

I really think that God has a sense of humor.
I'm here to tell you why.

When I make plans, I can hear God laugh.
In the end, *His* plans are *Divine*
and they supersede mine.

God already knows what I am destined to do.
He really knows what I want and need.
When I follow *His* plans, I will succeed.

God is the *Supreme Master* of this Universe.
No need to wonder what He expects of us.
It is spelled out in that special book.
Pick it up, open it up and take a look.

God has a sense of humor,
that may make you laugh or cry.
Just follow His commands and don't ask WHY.

Merry-Go-Round

Merry-Go-Round - Round and round it goes.

So much like life – the wise one knows.

Attempting to catch that illusive "Brass Ring".

So many seeking this catch as their daily thing.

Going in circles as the destination remains the same.

Creative imagination can produce a winning game.

So, Merry-Go-Round - Round and round it goes.

Enjoy this magical ride, with its high's and low's.

In Retrospect – We Can't and We Can

We can't unlive the past.
We can engage in retrospective thoughts.
We can't undo all wrongs.
We can seek needed forgiveness.
We can't prevent all accidents.
We can practice "Situational Awareness".
We can't see into the future.
We can learn from our past.
We can't be all things to all people.
We can help those who we can.
We can't change the whole world.
We can bring needed change where we live.
We can't read every book.
We can read the books that interest us.
We can't be a master of all things.
We can master our own unique talents.
We can't know what we can do until we try.
We can give things a try to see if we can.

We All Share One World

We all share one world,
with many races, colors and creeds.
We all share one moon,
for all to enjoy and see.
We all share one sun,
that shines equally for you and me.

The stars are placed in the universe,
to twinkle so eloquently.
Marvelous planets are in space,
though not visible to the naked eye.
They all serve a meaningful purpose,
being located between earth and sky.

Let's all join forces
to take care of our marvelous world.
It is not wise to take for granted
that it will always remain.
We owe it to our *Creator* to
preserve this precious gift.
Doing the right thing is up to me and you.

"Excuses"

I want to share a secret
that I know to be true.
Do not believe your "Excuses".
They will play a trick on you.

"Excuses" may throw some stumbling blocks
that creep into your head.
They can blind you to the truth
and make you stay in bed,

"Excuses" can make you lazy
and will hinder your success.
"Excuses" will hold you down
and keep you from doing your very best.

So, don't allow "Excuses"
to play such a forbidding game.
If you give in to "Excuses"
it would surely be a shame.

Razor Thin Ice

If you decide to skate on razor thin ice,
and ignore the posted signs,
know that if the ice breaks,
help may not immediately come your way.
Consequences may be difficult to endure,
but ignoring the signs will put you in danger for sure.

When putting ourselves in known harm's way,
God will still hear our cries,
but those who obey will tend to get *His*
more immediate response on any given day.

So, if you expect God to respond to your need for help,
abide by the posted signs
and beware of skating on razor thin ice.
This certainly is very wise lifesaving advice.

One Life to Live

We are all given one life to live.
Own it.

We are all given one life to live.
Live it well.

We are all given one life to live.
Live it now.

We are all given one live to live.
Preserve it.

We are all given one life to live.
Be grateful for it.

We are all given one life to live.
Seconds are not guaranteed.

Serenity Prayer

God grant me the serenity
to accept the things I cannot change;
courage to change the things I can;
and wisdom to know the difference.

Living one day at a time;
enjoying one moment at a time;
accepting hardships as the pathway to peace;
taking, as He did, this sinful world
as it is, not as I would have it:
trusting that He will make all things right
if I surrender to *His* Will;
that I may be reasonably happy in this life
and supremely happy with *Him*
forever in the next.
Amen
Reinhold Niebuhr (1892-1971)

Can Not Run – Can Not Hide

I can not run – I can not hide
from this person living inside.

They follow me all the time.
Where I go
they always know.

They peek inside
my every thought.
They even know what I was taught.

I have to always
do things right,
'cus I am always in their sight.

I have learned that
they will always be a part of me.
This has become my reality.

I can not run - I can not hide
from this person living inside.

My Five Senses at Work

I HEAR the voices of so many – in the distance –
    Crying out in undying pain.
There must be a way to calm the cries –
    To dull any need for future refrain.

I SEE the faces of too many – right up close –
    Painted with frowns of discontent.
There must be a way to ease the tensions –
    Bringing peace to those who are "over-spent".

I TASTE the bitterness of the nectar –
    Flowing from the flowers, covered with pollution.
There must be a way to cleanse the poison –
    Safely, peacefully – without a revolution.

I FEEL the sharpness of the thorns –
    That prick the innocent children at play.
There must be a way to remove the thorns –
    Keeping the children safe, by night and day.

I SMELL the sickening aroma of inner-city decay –
    Causing shallow breaths & oxygen deprivation to the brain.
There must be a way to purge the stench –
    With no dependence of clean-up by use of acid rain.

WE MUST CORRECT IT ALL IN THE NICK OF PRECIOUS TIME

A New Leaf

I awakened this morning.
I began reflecting on my life.
Needing some *Divine* guidance.
Seeking directions in minimizing strife.

The signs for needed changes
have appeared before my very eyes.
The signs did not play tricks
by appearing in a disguise.

I know it is time to 'turn over a new leaf',
as the old one has lost its life and luster.
I will welcome a fresh new foliage
and return of the energy I need to muster.

Color Me Selfish If You Will

Color me selfish if you will.
For a moment I must sit and chill.
Must roll back and slow the pace.
Got to get out of the hectic race.
Every problem will not be mine.
Can only take on those that I personally define.
Need to practice being wisely selective.
This is my way of being personally protective.
A brand "New Year" and a brand "New Life".
The intent is to minimize personal strife.
For a moment I must sit and chill.
Color me selfish if you will.

Oh, For Crying Out Loud

No more silent tears for me.
The sheer intensity of life
is causing me too much strife.

Oh, the ridged mountain is too high
for me to safely climb.
I have such a limited amount of time.

I've gotta find a real safe way
to escape the intensity of my emotional pain.
No longer a desire to even tell or explain.

Others may fail to understand
the profound feelings residing inside.
So, I keep it a secret to protect my pride.

The suppression of my feelings is a chore.
Please stop practicing 'man's inhumanity to man'.
Too many have their heads stuck in the sand.

Oh, For Crying Out Loud,
Unless we can agree to settle the score,
I can't take it anymore.

Speak It Into Existence

If you have a unique idea,
speak it into existence,
if you really want it to be.
Now, do the work to make it so.
Let your creative mind run free.

Don't allow anyone
to cast a shadow of doubt.
That even includes you.
For if you doubt yourself
you will not see your idea through.

There may be times
when you must take a break.
Just get back on track
and proceed for as long as it may take,

~~~~~~~~

**Speak it into existence.
Now, do the work to make it so.**

Pain

Pain is a jealous force
that over-takes its prey.
Pain gets our attention
in many cruel ways.
Pain can be relentless
and last for many days.

Giving it our full attention
will encourage it to stay.
We cannot allow it to
make us weaken and give in.
it can zap all our strength,
causing thoughts of recovery to end.

So, when pain attacks, call out all of the troops
to wage a winning war.
Gather all of the artillery needed
to annihilate the pain.
Use every available force
so that the pain will not remain.

The Weights of Life

The weights of life are heavy and rough
to my frail physique.

I'm struggling daily to carry these heavy loads
without falling to my knees.

Constantly seeking liberation
from these burdens that I am forced to carry.

Needed help is in very short supply.
Even those promising help, on them I can't rely.

The distance of my daily journey
is much longer than I had planned.

So, I'm not able to complete my list
of necessary chores that are expected of just me.

I need a <u>Magic Set of Hands</u> to lift
The Weights of Life
and free me from this pain.

I Asked God and He Gave

I asked to be rich, so that I could be happy.
He gave me less, so that I could be creative
and learn new survival skills.

I asked for power, so that others would praise me.
He gave me a common life
so that I would praise Him.

I asked for many extravagant earthly things
so that I would enjoy life.
He gave me life so that I could enjoy
the things that I have.

I asked for an over-abundance of wealthy friends.
He gave me a few true good friends
who would be there for me in times of need.

I asked for a mansion so that I could boast
about living in splendor.
He gave me a small dwelling so that I could feel
the closeness of family and friends.
~~~~~~~~~~~~~
I got nothing that I asked for but everything that I needed.

Whispers

Whispers of peace resonate in my mind,
reminding me that I must continue to be kind.

Whispers of joy spin around in my head,
reminding me to live a life without dread.

Whispers of harmony are performing
a symphony in my soul,
reminding me to include music as my daily goal.

Whispers of love have softly landed on my heart.
This is a tender reminder to appreciate
and embrace others like a work of precious art.
Whispers
Whispers
Whispers

No More Chasing Rainbows

No more chasing rainbows.
They are too very high in the sky.
The illusions of their beauty
have drawn me in for too long.
Must focus on other important things
and my decision must remain strong.

There are so many wonderful things
here on God's precious earth.
I shall focus on these things
that have meaning and perceived worth.

I shall continue to enjoy
those beautiful rainbows when they appear.
But no more chasing rainbows,
for their illusion will not draw me in.
This chase will not allow me to win.

Relax, Release, Unwind

Relax

Don't hold your fist so tight.
Open your hand and let life in.
You will receive so much greater joy.
Open your life and flow like the wind.

Release

Don't hold your fist so tight.
No holding back your love, time and gifts.
Release the tensions built up inside.
Let go of all of that needless pride..

Unwind

Don't hold your fist so tight.
Sit quietly and take time to exhale.
Unwind and you will find
much greater tranquility and peace of mind.

Ain't No Joke

Many things in life really ain't no joke.
Now I want to share some with my favorite folk.

- Dehydration is a serious matter.
  This is not just idle chatter.
- A severe pain in your side,
  that you should not ever hide.
- An aching head
  that puts you right to bed.
- Unexpected guest
  that won't let you get your rest.
- A bad performing car,
  that won't let you get too far.
- A bad tooth ache
  that keeps you awake.
- Not having enough money,
  No joke. It ain't funny.

~~~~~~

This could go on from here.
Even with a pain in your side, try to take it all in stride.

Keep the Music Playing

Keep the music playing, if only in your head.
Hear the melody playing to soothe your tender soul.
Create the unique lyrics from your treasured memories.

Keep the music playing to enhance your daily life.
Hear it smoothly playing, as you journey through your day.
Create the proper tempo to energize and refresh.

Keep the music playing as often as you wish.
Hear the fine-tuned orchestra, while you conduct your score.
Create the melodic music to instill personal harmony
and so much more.

Kindness Counts

Need to do your heart some good?
Kindness counts.

Need to do another some good?
Kindness counts.

Need to make a better life?
Kindness counts.

Need to make a heart grow fonder?
Kindness counts.

Need to break through a stretch of boredom?
Kindness counts.

Need to add joy to your day?
Kindness counts.

Need to create your personal rainbow?
Kindness to self and others really does count.

What If?

What if no one cares but me?
What if others don't see important things that I see?
What if I could get along but not go along?
What if I could make up my own bestselling song?
What if the world is not perfectly round?
What if I could invent something so profound?
What if I could tune out unwanted chatter?
What if I discover that gossip does not matter?
What if I could connect the dots and stop crime?
What if the cure for cancer would only cost a dime?
What if equal education would be embraced by all?
What if I could feel safe going to the mall?
What if calories could all be pre-set at zero?
What if I could discover a way to become a hero?
What If?   What If?   What If?

Only Time Will Tell

We know not what tomorrow will really bring.
Only time will tell.

We know not what is in store for us.
Only time will tell.

We know not what we may be called on to do.
Only time will tell.

We know not what each season will bring.
Only time will tell.

We know not how the story will end.
Only time will tell.
~~~~~~
Give it time to find out and then we will know.

Will Be Silent No More

I have a voice to speak the truth.
Will no longer keep my truth within.

The things that have been done to me,
will be shared with others who need to know.

I owe it to others the secrets to reveal,
that should have been done long ago.

I was too embarrassed to be a part
of their "cruel commanding game".
No longer am I accepting the blame.
Nor am I willing to live with the shame.

~~~~~~~~~

Will Be Silent No More

Show Me the Way Lord

Grab me by the hand Lord and please show me the way.
My body is in pain and the pain won't go away.
Pill after pill ain't doing me any good.
Others don't seem to understand.
I really wish that they would.
Don't want to continue to live like this.
Some think I'm too addicted to make a change.
I do want help and someone to show me the way.

Don't want to show my face that no longer looks like me.
My eyes, my skin, my teeth, my hair are all looking worn.
Lord, the pain and the drugs have taken their toll.
I've lost my youth and looking so very old.
Wish that I could roll back the hands of "Father Time".
I want to relive the life of my innocent youth.
Not blaming anyone but I need to tell the truth..
Help ain't found in a bottle, a pill or hypodermic needle.
Of all these things, I've already tried.

I know that I'm worth giving another chance to live pain free.
There are so many others needing help just like me.
Please grab us all by the hand Lord and show us the way.
I'm pleading for your hand Lord........Please do it today!!!!

Please Hear Our Cries

Oppression – Suppression – Recession – Depression

Pressing down on the very soul,
leads to depression and lack of self-control.
Those special tools needed to restore and uplift,
is a much-needed special gift.

....

Oppression
Suppression
Recession
Escalating Depression

....

Division
Subtraction
Addition
Multiplication to the Rescue

....

Less Human <u>Division</u>
<u>Subtraction</u> of Hatred
<u>Addition</u> of Much Deeper Love
<u>Multiplication</u> of Generosity and Empathy

....

Cure Oppression, Suppression, Recession, Depression!

Too Afraid to Ask

Sometimes when I need help
I'm too afraid to ask.
My personal need for help appears
to be getting in the way.
Some come across as if
they are having a bad day.

If only I could manage
I would do things for myself.
The condition that I now have
has set me back a spell.
The feelings that are hiding out inside,
I do not want to tell.

So, when I ask for help,
please have empathy and respect.
Please don't make me feel like
I'm not even worth what I pay.
If you only knew how hard it is
to depend on another to help make my day.

....

Note: This poem expresses the feelings of my husband
who resided in a series of senior care facilities.

Plowing the Fields of Life

There is no doubt that living in today's climate of discontent and uncertainty is challenging for many of us. It feels as if there is a vast field that needs to be cultivated and we need a sharp and rugged plow to accomplish the tasks. If the field is too vast, we need "Field Hands" to help. Do we decide to cultivate a smaller field if the needed resources are not available? There are always decisions to be made as we navigate our daily lives.

Sometimes we need to cut back on the workload and focus on cultivating a smaller crop for a season. We are the decision maker, and it is up to us to identify the various seasons of our lives. As we advance in age and as certain limitations are placed on us, it is important to evaluate how many tasks we should commit to and/or how large or field should be.

Stress is a danger to our physical, mental, emotional, spiritual and financial health. When we over-stress ourselves by taking on more than we can handle, and allow ourselves to be subjected to prolonged stressors, this impacts our well-being.

It is important to periodically take time to evaluate the size of your 'field' and determine the quality of the harvest. Evaluate the seasons of your life and make a conservative plan to make necessary changes. Listen to that inner voice. Listen to the messenger of reason.

Triggers for Anger, Rage and/or Antagonism

The following is a short and conservative list of situations that may cause people to lose control of their behavior. In doing so, they become angry, enraged and/or antagonistic. Bringing an awareness to the following situations may help to identify those things and mitigate the need to engage in such negative behavior. We may ask God to "Hear our cries" but God needs something from us. It is important that we live our lives within the guidelines of 'God's Laws' and 'Man's Laws'. We also need to be aware of and practice other factors that contribute to a civil society.

The following are triggers for anger, rage and/or antagonism:
1. Lack of education, information and/or good communication skills
2. Inferiority complex
3. Unfavorable experiences (from childhood through adulthood)
4. Lack of information and/or role models for how to deal with anger and confrontations
5. Being economically deprived
6. Feeling detached, ignored and/or neglected
7. Feeling misunderstood
8. Rough treatment and/or feeling manipulated
9. Unfair judgment and/or being wrongly accused
10. Lack of a spiritual connection
11. Lack of an identifiable purpose
12. Feeling trapped, threatened and/or framed
13. Oppression and/or harassment
14. Lack of survival skills
15. Lack of basic resources
16. Fears (including fear of failure or even of success)
17. Lack of problem-solving skills
18. Identity crisis (confused about their gender assignment)
19. Lack of hope and/or lack of trust
20. Dysfunctional families
21. Dysfunctional communities

22. Unwanted isolation
23. Feeling crushed and emotionally broken
24. Failed support system
25. Drugs, alcohol and/or other substance abuse
26. Wanting more out of life
27. Medical and chemical imbalances
28. Feeling dehumanized, worthless and/or defeated (beyond redemption)
29. Lack of compassion for others and/or lack of humility
30. Encountering bigotry and racial bias
31. Feeling unloved and/or unlovable
32. Inflated ego, vane and/or self-centered personalities
33. Lack of internal peace, self-respect and/or the ability for having self-control

Write You Own Thoughts

Things That Bring Me Joy

Write Your Own Thoughts

Things That Cause Me Sadness

Write Your Own Thoughts

Things Live in My Memory Bank

Write You Own Thoughts

Things That Amaze Me

Write Your Own Thoughts

Things That I Hope for the Future

Write Your Own Thoughts

Things That Turn Me Off

Write Your Own Thoughts

Things That Turn Me Own

Write Your Own Thoughts

Things That the World Needs Now

Write Your Own Thoughts

Things That Keep Me on My Toes

Write Your Own Thoughts

Things That I Would Do with A Million Dollars

Write Your Own Thoughts

Things That I Need to Get Off My Chest

Write Your Own Thoughts

My Favorite Season of the Year and Why

Write Your Own Thoughts

My Favorite Holiday and Why

Write Your Own Thoughts

My Biggest Accomplishments

Write Your Own Thoughts

What I Admire About Myself

Write Your Own Thoughts

What I Would Change About Myself

Write Your Own Thoughts

What I Wish Someone Would Do for Me

Write Your Own Thoughts

What I Admire About My Best Friend

Write Your Own Thoughts

A Habit That I Need to Break

Write Your Own Thoughts

A Secret That I Am Ready to Share

Write Your Own Thoughts

The People Who Have Inspired Me

~~~~~~~~~~~~~~~~

~~~~~~~

~~~~~~~~~~~~~~~~~~